Best Holiday Ever
By Celia and Orison Carlile

First edition published 2015

Dedicated to all parents who have taken
their children on holidays.

We would like to acknowledge Aaron O'Driscoll
for his technical support.

BEST HOLIDAY EVER

By Celia and Orison Carlile

Hi, this is my holiday album and I'm going to tell you about the best holiday ever.

We got up early and were ready in plenty of time to head off to the airport.

Our car →

When we got to the airport
Dad found a lovely parking
place and we headed for
the terminal.

Our flight was very smooth.

Our luggage had gone to a different airport. I did not know that bags could have their own holiday.

The taxi did not take long to get to the hotel.

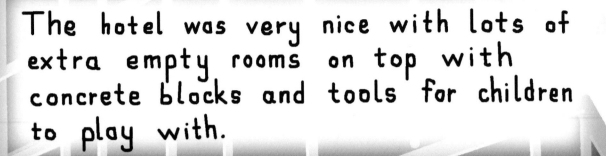

The hotel was very nice with lots of extra empty rooms on top with concrete blocks and tools for children to play with.

HOTEL INCOMPLETO

They had charity shops just like at home. We bought lots of lovely clothes to wear while our real clothes were on their holidays.

I loved the foreign food. It was far more interesting than the boring stuff we have at home.

After the meal we all went on a sight-seeing trip to the local hospital. Mummy got some souvenir medicine there. She allowed me to carry it for her. From the label I learned how to spell 'diarrhoea'. It is a cool word.

Mummy really loved the bathroom in our hotel. She even said her prayers there.

Mum was feeling
better next day
so we went to
the beach. Dad
was able to beat
a fish in a race.

Mum got great exercise too. She had fun chasing a new friend who borrowed her handbag for a while.

Meanwhile we children went for a lovely trip on an air mattress. There were lovely fish all around us.

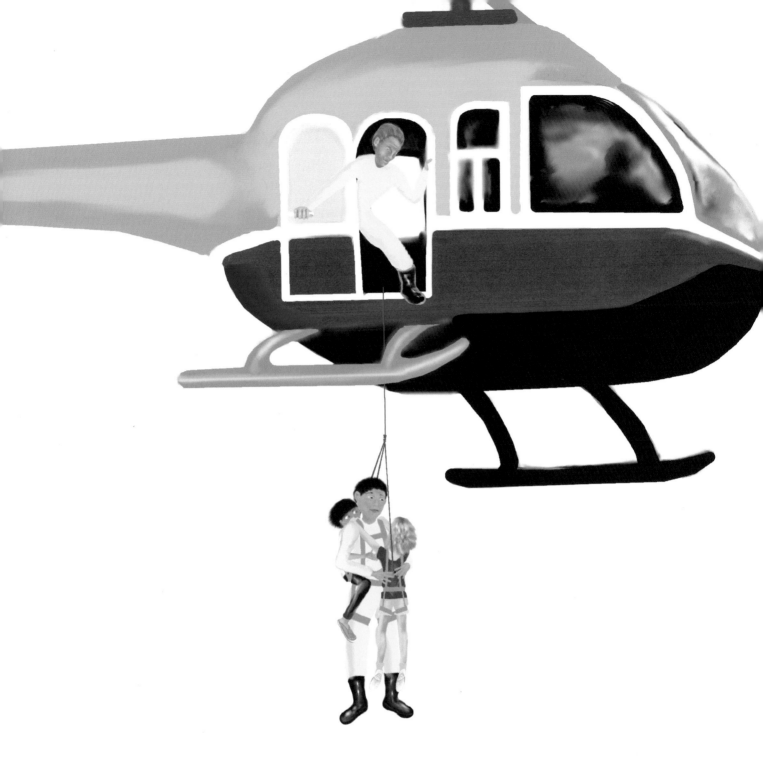

Then it got even better as we got a ride in a helicopter.

Then we went on the rides.

We went horse riding. Dad did tricks like in a circus.

On the last day of our holidays we went shopping for souvenirs. I bought a toy gun and slipped it into Dad's pocket as a surprise.

The flight home was just as good as the flight over.

After we landed we found our car. It did not take the tow truck long to roll it over onto its side.

On the way home, Mum and Dad said that we would never go on a holiday like that again. I agree because it was the best holiday ever.

Hear the song at celiacarlile.com

- The Best Holiday Ever -

Words: Orison Carlile

Music: Rob Carlile